Books by Eleanor Berry

The Story of Paddy (A pornographic book – not published)
Tell Us a Sick One Jakey (Out of print)
Never Alone with Rex Malone (Out of print)
Someone's Been Done Up Harley
O, Hitman, My Hitman!
The Adventures of Eddy Vernon
Stop the Car, Mr Becket! (Formerly *The Rendon Boy to the Grave Is Gone*)
Robert Maxwell as I Knew Him (Out of print)
Cap'n Bob and Me (Out of print)
McArandy Was Hanged on the Gibbet High
The House of the Weird Doctors
Sixty Funny Stories
The Most Singular Adventures of Sarah Lloyd
Alandra Varinia – Sarah's Daughter
The Rise and Fall of Mad Silver Jaxton
By the Fat of Unborn Leopards
The Killing of Lucinda Maloney
My Old Pal Was a Junkie (Available in Russian)
Your Father Had to Swing, You Little Bastard! (Also available in Russian)
An Eye for a Tooth and a Limb for an Eye
Help Me, Help Me, It's Red!
Come Sweet Sexton, Tend My Grave
My Face Shall Appear on the Banknotes
My Unique Relationship with Robert Maxwell – The Truth at Last
My Father Was a Newspaper Man
Too Much Bloody Noise
Dr Ted Curruthers & Dr Isaac Stone

Reviews

Tell Us a Sick One Jakey
'This book is quite repulsive!' Sir Michael Havers, Attorney General

Never Alone with Rex Malone
'A ribald, ambitious black comedy, a story powerfully told.' Stewart Steven, *The Daily Mail*

'I was absolutely flabbergasted when I read it!' *Robert Maxwell*

Robert Maxwell as I Knew Him
'One of the most amusing books I have read for a long time. Eleanor Berry is an original.' Elisa Segrave, *The Literary Review*

'Undoubtedly the most amusing book I have read all year.' Julia Llewellyn-Smith, *The Times*

'With respect and I repeat, with very great respect, because I know you're a lady, but all you ever do is just go on and on and on and on about this bleeding bloke!' *Reggie Kray*

Cap'n Bob and Me
'A comic masterpiece.' *The Times*

'As befits the maternal granddaughter of F.E. Smith (famous barrister who never lost a case) Eleanor Berry has a sharp tone of phrase and a latent desire for upsetting people. Campaigning for her hero, Robert Maxwell, in a General Election, she climbed to the top of the Buckingham Town Hall and erected the red flag. Eleanor Berry fits into the long tradition of British eccentricity.' Stewart Graham, *The Spectator*

Someone's Been Done Up Harley
'Eleanor Berry's dazzling wit hits the Harley Street scene. Her extraordinary humour had me in stitches.' Thelma Masters, *The Oxford Times*

O, Hitman, My Hitman!
'Eleanor Berry's volatile pen is at it again. This time, she takes her readers back to the humorously eccentric Harley Street community. She also introduces Romany gypsies and travelling circuses, a trait which she has inherited from her self-confessed gypsy aunt, the late writer, Eleanor Smith, after whom she was named. Like Smith, Berry is an inimitable and delightfully natural writer.' Kev Zein, *The Johannesburg Evening Sketch*

McArandy Was Hanged on the Gibbet High
'We have here a potboiling, swashbuckling blockbuster, which is rich in adventure, intrigue, history, amorous episodes and above all black humour. The story Eleanor Berry tells is multi-coloured, multi-faceted and nothing short of fantastic.' Angel Z. Hogan, *The Daily Melbourne Times*

The Adventures of Eddy Vernon
'Rather a hot book for bedtime.' The late Nigel Dempster, *The Daily Mail*

Stop the Car, Mr Becket! (formerly *The Rendon Boy to the Grave Is Gone*)
'This book makes for fascinating reading, as strange, black-humoured and entertaining as Eleanor Berry's other books which came out before it.' Gaynor Evans, *Bristol Evening Post*

Sixty Funny Stories
'This book is a laugh a line.' Elisa Segrave, writer and diarist

The House of the Weird Doctors
'This delightful medical caper puts even A.J. Cronin in the shade.' Noel I. Leskin, *The Stethoscope*

The Most Singular Adventures of Sarah Lloyd
'A riotous read from start to finish.' Ned McMurphy, *The Irish Times*

Alandra Varinia – Sarah's Daughter
'Eleanor Berry manages to maintain her raw and haunting wit as much as ever.' Dwight C. Farr, *The Texas Chronicle*

The Rise and Fall of Mad Silver Jaxton
'This time, Eleanor Berry tries her versatile hand at politics. Her sparkling wit and the reader's desire to turn the page are still in evidence. Eleanor Berry is unique.' Don F. Saunderson, *The South London Review*

'This is a dark, disturbing but at the same time hilarious tale of a megalomaniac dictator by the always readable and naughty Eleanor Berry.' The late Sally Farmiloe, award-winning actress and author

By the Fat of Unborn Leopards
'Could this ribald, grisly-humoured story about a right-wing British newspaper magnate's daughter, possibly be autobiographical, by any chance?' Peggy-Lou Kadinsky, *The Washington Globe*

'Fantastically black. A scream from beginning to end.' Charles Kidd, Editor of *Debrett's Peerage*

The Killing of Lucinda Maloney
'This is the funniest book I've read for months.' Samantha Morris, *The Exeter Daily News*

My Old Pal Was a Junkie
'Eleanor Berry is to literature what Hieronymus Bosch is to art. As with all Miss Berry's books, the reader has a burning urge to turn the page.' Sonia Drew, *The Texas Times*

Your Father Had to Swing, You Little Bastard!
'A unique display of black humour which somehow fails to depress the reader.' Craig McLittle, *The Rugby Gazette*

'This book is an unheard of example of English black humour. Eleanor Berry is almost a reincarnation of our own beloved Dostoevsky.' Sergei Robkov, Russian magazine, *Minuta*

An Eye for a Tooth and a Limb for an Eye
'Words are Eleanor Berry's toys and her use of them is boundless.' Mary Hickman, professional historian and writer

Help Me, Help Me, It's Red!
'Despite the sometimes weighty portent of this book, a sense of subtle, dry and black humour reigns throughout its pages. The unexpected twist is stupendous.' Stephen Carson, *The Carolina Sun*

'This is grim humour at its very best. The most challenging and most delightful novel I have read in six months.' Scott Mason-Jones, *The New York Globe*

Come, Sweet Sexton, Tend My Grave
'Breathtakingly black, a treasure to read from beginning to end.' Grace Ponsonby, *Newsweek*

My Face Shall Appear on the Banknotes
'Tightly paced and bitter-sweet throughout.' Alexis Lawrence, *The Cork Evening News*

'A satisfying and fantastic read in all ways.' George Cullen

My Unique Relationship with Robert Maxwell – The Truth at Last
'A scholarly, moving but at the same time, delightfully comic work, seeped in black humour – a genuine page-turner. This is the most entertaining book, I have read so far about the controversial Mirror Magnate and Eleanor Berry's friendship with him. So far we have only heard negative things about him, but Eleanor has shown his human, kind and compassionate side, hitherto unknown to the British public.' John Cohen, *The Oxford Times*

Tell My Son to Make Peace With His Forefathers
and the Involvement of Natalie Klein

Eleanor Berry

The Book Guild Ltd

First published in Great Britain in 2024 by
The Book Guild Ltd
Unit E2 Airfield Business Park,
Harrison Road, Market Harborough,
Leicestershire. LE16 7UL
Tel: 0116 2792299
www.bookguild.co.uk
Email: info@bookguild.co.uk
X: @bookguild

Copyright © 2024 Eleanor Berry

The right of Eleanor Berry to be identified as the author of this
work has been asserted by them in accordance with the
Copyright, Design and Patents Act 1988.

All rights reserved. No part of this publication may be
reproduced, transmitted, or stored in a retrieval system, in any form or by any means,
without permission in writing from the publisher, nor be otherwise circulated in
any form of binding or cover other than that in which it is published and without
a similar condition being imposed on the subsequent purchaser.

This work is entirely fictitious and bears no resemblance to any persons living or dead.

Typeset in 11pt Baskerville

Printed on FSC accredited paper
Printed and bound in Great Britain by 4edge Limited

ISBN 978 1835740 224

British Library Cataloguing in Publication Data.
A catalogue record for this book is available from the British Library.

To a beautiful psychiatrist and a beautiful lover

It was Harley Street (sometimes known as "Swindlestrasse"). It was a Friday afternoon. A blonde woman called Natalie Klein was dressed in clinging black leather and mounted the steps, leading to a building, and rang the bell. A psychiatrist wearing pinstripe trousers, opened the door.

"I'm having a lot of trouble, getting BBC Two. Can you please send someone out, to fix my television? I'll be without a television for the whole weekend, and I particularly want to watch a programme on BBC Two," said the woman curtly.

The psychiatrist, a tall, slim, balding figure of a man, stared at the woman, and the woman stared at the psychiatrist. He had small, grey, piercing eyes, and she had large, brown, searching eyes. He leant curiously against the shiny, black door, which said "Number 12".

"I am a psychiatrist," he said eventually. His voice was quiet and low, and his intonation was slow.

Unlike his, her voice was loud and penetrating.

"You circumcised?" asked the woman casually.

The psychiatrist looked askance at her.

"Yes, as a matter of fact, I am." His tone of voice was reluctant and embarrassed.

"Jolly Hockey Sticks!" There was a pause. She added, "In that case, we will go into your consulting room, and use your leather-studded couch. I like my lovers to be snipped."

"What name is it?" asked the psychiatrist timidly.

"Natalie Klein."

"My name is Mortimer Schatzman."

Afterwards, Dr Schatzman slammed the door in Natalie's face and was replaced by a rosy-cheeked receptionist.

"I need several psychiatrists," said Natalie, vaguely.

"We only need one psychiatrist and his name is Jesus," said the receptionist bizarrely.

***

Natalie Klein was unlike other women. She was in her thirties and lived in Golders Green, with her housekeeper, Rhoda. She liked to wear leather suits of different colours, leopard-skin printed polo-necked sweaters, and carried a leopard-skin printed handbag.

Her house was of reasonable size, and red brick, and she got on well with her neighbours, whom she saw regularly, mainly for tea. She had dyed blonde hair, large brown eyes and was about five foot four inches tall.

She hailed from a large, literary London-based family, and like all members of her family, was a prolific writer. Her father was a newspaper proprietor. She specialised exclusively in black-humoured novels, because that mode of writing alleviated her occasional melancholy fits. She was also a hypochondriac, and lived on a cacophony of pills, like her mother.

Her tastes in men were also prolific. She had a *penchant* for top Harley Street psychiatrists, who wore tight trousers and whom she paid extortionately for their sexual services.

Her favourite Harley Street psychiatrist, whom she employed in this way, was Dr Ted Carruthers, and he had long since died. She was gutted by his death. Not only that, she had paid him far more than the other psychiatrists.

She was a pathological exhibitionist and boasted to her friends and neighbours about her sexual behaviour. She also liked to state the amounts of money she had inherited from Saul Klein, her wealthy grandfather, whose portrait hung in her oak-panelled dining room.

Saul was a prominent politician and statesman. He was fonder of Natalie than her brothers and sister, because she had paid more attention to him, throughout his long life. He died in Natalie's arms, and, like his granddaughter, he wrote one book after another, while sitting in his oak-panelled study.

Like Natalie, he favoured macabre themes in his prose, but unlike his granddaughter, he preferred to write biographies, rather than novels.

Saul died in his bedroom on a Sunday afternoon, and Natalie wept profusely. She decided to sleep in her grandfather's bed, to begin with, in order to soak up his spirit.

Rhoda, his housekeeper and cook, as well, wept in his bedroom. Rhoda was delighted when Natalie asked her to continue her employ, and even more delighted when she found out that Saul, an exceptionally generous man, had left her a considerable amount in his will.

By far the greatest amount of Saul's legacy went to Natalie. She was close to her late brothers and her sister,

Hilary, and bribed the Klein family's lawyers not to disclose the amount left to her by Saul. It is not known how she managed to do this, however.

Natalie employed a chauffeur, called Jones, who bought clothing for her psychiatrists, other lovers and, in particular for the late Carruthers, a desperate man, whose evil wife had thrown all his suits into a field.

Many of Natalie's psychiatrists were different in size and height, so Jones carried a tape measure in his pocket. He visited shops and consulting rooms, measured the sizes of their trousers and shirts, and even did this when their patients were lying on their leather-studded couches.

Many of Natalie's psychiatrists liked to show off, just as much as Natalie did. She also liked these men to be snipped, as she stated before, and made a point of telling her friends and neighbours this, so that she could get the audiences she craved.

Some of her friends and neighbours came to tea about once a week. Natalie moved the candelabra to one side, so that she could get a glimpse of her handsome grandfather, while she spoke at length about her adventures.

***

The phone rang. One of Natalie's neighbours, Mrs Sarah Goulding, was on the line and in a state of extreme distress. Mrs Goulding was to play a significant part in Natalie's later life.

Later that evening, Sarah appeared even more agitated and insisted that Natalie accompany her to the nearest pub. Sarah was about sixty or so. She was sitting in a dark corner of the room, and Natalie sat opposite her. The younger woman ordered a double gin and tonic and treated her companion to the same amount.

Sarah was wearing a dark navy-blue dress, and her tear-stained eyes were large and bright blue. She was browsing casually through the *Financial Times*.

"You seem to be in trouble," said Natalie kindly, while the older woman wept. "As you are aware, I spend most of my time writing books, novels, mainly." She added, "They are all black comedies. I write for posterity."

"My name is Sarah, as you know. There is only one thing in the world that I yearn to achieve and one thing only."

"Which is what, Sarah?" asked Natalie.

"I want my fifteen-year-old son, and only relative, to make his peace with his father. One thing I can't bear in life, is loneliness."

Sarah was even more tearful, and because weeping was natural to her, she went on doing so.

"Where is your son at the moment, and what is his name?" asked Natalie, sympathetically.

"His name is Moshe," said the older woman. "He is living in a damp bedsit in Stoke Newington, incidentally, where the poet, Edgar Allan Poe, went to school. My son has lived there for most of his life.

"He won't live with me. He likes to lie on his back, doing absolutely nothing, except stare at the ceiling. I want to move him to a more suitable place, preferably to Israel, near his father's grave," said Sarah. "It would be very nice if we could go to Israel together."

"I'd like that," said Natalie. "I haven't got anything to do."

It took the two women at least an hour to drive from Golders Green to Moshe's dreary bedsit in Stoke Newington. Moshe was wearing a shabby dark dressing gown, and watching a small black-and-white television, with the sound turned down, and his eyes vacantly crossed. Sarah introduced Natalie to him, and said they were neighbours.

"Come on, my boy!" added Sarah impatiently. "Wash yourself and get dressed. There's a limousine outside, waiting to take us to London airport. We're getting a plane to Tel Aviv, so that you will be able to visit your father's grave in the Valley of the Blessed in Jerusalem. I've got the tickets."

Moshe was startled. He washed slowly and pulled on his only clothes which were shabby and grey, like his dressing gown. He took his mother's arm, as well as Natalie's, and shambled down the dangerous, rickety, stairs.

It was raining hard, and the driver hired to take them to the airport, was surly and silent throughout the journey. Nor did he open the doors for his passengers or make any effort to help them with their luggage.

"Thanks for helping us with our luggage! Don't expect me to tip you, boy!" shouted Sarah, who had said nothing during the journey, other than passing the odd remark about the rain.

The trio boarded the plane bound for Tel Aviv. Moshe, his spirits a trifle higher, skipped as he mounted the gangplank, like an adolescent. No one would have thought that he was fifteen years old.

"Do you know why I want to take you on this journey?" asked Sarah, once more.

"I've got a vague idea," replied Moshe. "Besides, I don't want to live in a dark, damp room, looking at a ceiling anymore. It really has been making me feel very depressed over the years."

Natalie changed the subject.

"What is your full name?" she asked the boy.

"Moshe Isaac Goulding," Moshe replied. "I have the same surname as my mother has and the same middle name as my father."

Sarah spoke once more, "My husband's grave is occupied by one who has served the Jewish people in many different ways, particularly during World War II, and who is a major hero among the British people."

"Where will we be staying?" asked the boy.

"In the King David Hotel, where guests are the most important and richest in the world," replied Sarah, adding reverently, "I have arranged for a guide to take us to the graveyard tomorrow morning. He will help us, once we arrive, so that we can make our way over the graves until we reach your father's grave."

"You really are talking an awful lot, Mother," said Moshe, impertinently, "but do go on."

"I have met our guide before," said the interrupted mother. "His name is Aaron Epstein. It will be hot tomorrow morning, and I hope he will be able to provide us with cold drinks from a kiosk outside the graveyard."

"Are you looking forward to visiting the Valley of the Blessed, Moshe?" asked Natalie.

"Yes. Anything would be better than the place I've been living in at the moment, as I said before."

For some reason, the air conditioning on the plane had

broken down, although the trio had been able to enjoy films. Natalie had become very hot, however, but Sarah and Moshe had become pleasantly cool. Sarah took out her tapestry, showing an old biblical scene, which she began to work on.

"Our story started a long time ago," she said in an embarrassed tone, "Isaac, my husband, and I, had a daughter called Ruth, who was much younger than Moshe. Ruth was run over, when she went out to buy sweets one day." Sarah added, "Isaac and I were heartbroken."

Natalie didn't know how to deal with people who were gutted. She stroked the older woman's hand.

***

The flight to Tel Aviv lasted for at least another hour or so. During that time, Sarah, Moshe and Natalie did what they could to take advantage of what few films were available.

Their passage through Customs was uneventful, as was the taxi ride to the luxurious hotel arranged by Sarah. An air-conditioned limousine collected the party the following morning and drove them to the Valley of the Blessed. It was there that they met Aaron Epstein, their guide.

On reaching the grave, the three travellers stood motionless, and Sarah laid large stones on top of her husband's grave. Epstein lit some candles and placed them around the stones.

Moshe remembered his distant childhood. When his mother had misguidedly taken him to his father's funeral at the age of about ten, there were a number of photographers surrounding the grave.

The boy was very shy and jumped over the headstone, before throwing more stones into the distance, and at the bemused photographers.

Even at the age of fifteen, Moshe felt ashamed of his previous behaviour. Sarah felt less ashamed, however, and suddenly broke into song. Her singing was sublime and even divine in places. There was something distinctly Hebrew about it. She had temporarily felt distressed but nostalgic at the same time.

"That was a wonderful song, Mother," Moshe exclaimed. Natalie had never heard the song before, and felt close to tears, despite the heat. Spontaneously, she sang *Hava Nagila*, the only Hebrew song she knew.

"I bet they never taught you to sing songs like that at your school," said Sarah, turning to her son.

The young man paused. "No, I'm afraid they didn't," he said, adding, "All they taught us to sing was boring old songs, like, *All Things Bright and Beautiful* and *Old MacDonald had a Farm*. It's quite clear that you sent me to the wrong school, Mother."

"I'm so sorry, my boy. I certainly sent you to the wrong school," agreed Sarah guiltily.

Natalie smiled self-consciously. Her parents had sent her to a public school, and enabled her to be well educated, before she went to university.

"Have you got any cassettes of the wonderful song you sang just then, Sarah?" she asked.

"Unfortunately, not. I wish I had. We had a burglary, and almost everything was stolen."

***

Aaron laid some more large stones on Moshe's father's grave, and lit some more candles round the stones, before praying out loud. Neither Sarah, nor Natalie, nor Mosche understood the prayers.

It was at that time that Sarah decided to teach her son Hebrew, and to learn the language herself. Moshe began to wear dreadlocks, like other Jewish boys, and felt as one with them. He visited his father's grave regularly, once he had learned the difficult language.

Although the mother and son had immersed themselves in the study of fluent Hebrew, Natalie had not, and hated the permanent, and unvaryingly hot weather. She told Sarah that she intended to return to London, and that she would visit the older woman and her son on a regular basis.

She went back to her house in Golders Green and joined Rhoda, who was delighted by her company.

Sarah had already moved into a small, white-walled flat, which she shared with Moshe. The windows were tiny. When the boy asked a taxi driver why the windows were so small, he replied, "We have to keep out the Palestinians!"

"Fucking Palestinians!" muttered the boy.

"Language, Moshe!" muttered Sarah.

Natalie corresponded regularly with Sarah and Moshe, but she still saw her friends in London, on a frequent basis. She was very gregarious. Many of them were from her schools. Many were from university. Others she had met before, when she was in prison, and most of all, she made a considerable number of friends while canvassing during general elections.

Apart from contact with all these people, she embarked on commercial translation, using French and Russian, and when this eventually bored her, she started to work as a medical secretary.

Medical secretarial work fascinated her. London agencies sent her from one hospital to another, in which she worked from department to department. Eventually, she worked in the Nephrology Department at St Bartholomew's Hospital, otherwise known as "Barts". This department specialised in renal medicine, that is to say, the study of the kidneys.

Once she had settled, she was confined to a cosy attic, overlooking one of the domes of the Old Bailey. The attic let in the sun for most of the day.

She shared the attic with another medical secretary. Each secretary was different in her ways, and each had her own personality about her.

Natalie first shared the attic with a woman called Doris, her best friend. For some reason, Doris refused to reveal her husband's occupation, because she thought he was beneath her socially. It turned out that he was a black cab driver. Natalie didn't find out his occupation until Doris's funeral and was very surprised by the way Doris had covered his occupation. She thought he was in the IRA, at first.

Doris suffered from pulmonary fibrosis. Gradually, her breathing became worse and worse. Eventually, she had to carry a metal lung on her back, like an aqualung.

Natalie took Doris out to dinner every night, and bonked the metal lung onto the tables, in a theatrical manner, to induce what humour she could. She was gutted when Doris died, in an outer London hospital.

Her next office companion was called Rita, a fiery Irish woman from Dublin. Natalie and Rita had a love-hate relationship.

Eventually, Rita, who did not take precautions, because she was a Catholic, became pregnant, and married an Arab from Dubai. She hadn't been heard of since.

Rita was replaced by a woman, known throughout the hospital, as "Stinker", who was depressingly genteel. Natalie opened the mail with a flick knife, and "Stinker" said, each time, with a pronounced lisp, "My husband, who is a policeman, says it's illegal to carry a flick knife." "Stinker" got on Natalie's nerves, every time she opened the mail.

She finally got rid of "Stinker" by telling tales about her and showing senior doctors her appallingly bad photocopies. Also, "Stinker" resented Natalie's daily phone conversations, with Moshe and Sarah. Moshe was growing up and loved to talk to Natalie at length.

The boy was already in a more senior school in Jerusalem and had a large number of friends. He had also made friends with a girl the same age as him, and he intended to introduce her to his mother.

The girl was an orthodox Jewess called Rachel. Sarah was afraid of their getting married and causing his mother the loneliness that she had suffered earlier in her life.

Natalie assured Sarah that the liaison might not necessarily result in the raising of a large family. "Stinker" complained bitterly yet again about Natalie's frequent personal phone calls, and often slapped down the receiver.

"You're not supposed to make personal phone calls," she said. "I've told you this before."

"That's none of your fucking business!" said Natalie. "The calls often come through to me, not the other way round.

"Besides, I've already shown your terrible photocopies to some of the senior doctors. In most instances, it's not possible to see the names of the patients concerned or the doctors either." Natalie added, "Another thing, don't ever slap the receiver down when a call is coming through. It's considered bad manners."

Natalie found out that "Stinker" was proverbially allergic to garlic, so she smothered her breath with large quantities of garlic.

"Stinker" told what few friends she had, about this terrible problem, and couldn't stop talking about it to her wretched husband. She spoke about it during dinner, during breakfast, and even in the car, driving her to the hospital.

Her husband told her that he was so fed up with hearing about Natalie Klein, that he intended to divorce her, on grounds of boredom. He frequently went to his local after dinner, to join his mates, and returned to his house late at night. "Stinker" was almost asleep by this time but was willing to approach the dreaded subject of Natalie's garlic yet again.

In the end, the policeman insisted on sleeping in their spare room, and even his mates in the pub avoided his company. Husband and wife eventually separated, and "Stinker" became even more unhappy than she had been before.

***

Natalie had another problem, however. This was due to the attitude of the chief consultant in her department. His name was Donald Greenwood and he had fallen in love with her. He was perilously ugly, and always wore a white coat, which was at least two sizes too small for him, making him look ridiculous.

His face was bright red, suggesting, either that he had too much to drink on a permanent basis, or that he suffered from raised blood pressure. Also, he had terrible body odour.

His love for Natalie was of a particularly possessive nature and became worse as the weeks went by. She told him that she had a regular boyfriend, but Greenwood's love for her turned to hatred, like that of a woman spurned.

It did not take him long to find plenty of reasons to sack her. His main motive was the frequency of her personal phone calls, which he had overlooked earlier.

He also noticed the collection of flick knives in her top drawer, as well as that of pornographic photographs in the same place. Although he never found anything wrong with her typing, which had been impeccable at all times, he sat gloomily at his desk for hours on end, deep in thought and desperate to fault her work in some way or another.

The only other thing he could think of, of an adverse nature, was her outrageously loud voice, which he claimed upset the patients on a regular basis.

None of these plans worked, as Natalie's so-called offences were not provocative enough. However, the vindictive doctor was a heroin addict, and left a sachet of heroin in her top drawer, where she kept her flick knives. There was evidence of the drug in her possession, and she was asked to appear before a panel, before being sacked.

As was her wont, Natalie took what she called "Churchillian revenge" on Greenwood. She hired a private detective, to find the cause of the injustice committed towards her.

Her first move was to send the doctor anonymous leaflets on impotence and premature ejaculation. These were to be sent to his office, so that other members of his staff could see them.

She also sent representatives of the Communist Party to his private lodgings. These people do not actually cause injury. They are like wasps, buzzing round and round a plate, and stay for hours on end.

A further form of revenge, which she took, was the sending of Jehovah's Witnesses to Greenwood's house. The first of Natalie's typed letters read as follows: "Please send someone round to my house, late at night, so that we can have a long discussion about Christ."

Dr Greenwood had a nervous breakdown. He had no idea who had sent these missiles.

***

Natalie's agency then sent her to the secretariat in the chest department, at the Whittington Hospital in Highgate. The agency's administrator, John Tabb, was familiar with Dr Greenwood's predatory habits and deviousness. He also knew about Natalie's exemplary typing.

The atmosphere in her new office was more relaxed, the food in the canteen was more edible than that at Barts, and the staff were much nicer to her. Also, the consultants failed to make passes at her, and appreciated her unblemished typing.

The hospital was loosely attached to a women's prison, whose inmates frequently visited the chest department.

They suffered profusely from chest disease, and crashed onto the premises, handcuffed to wardens or screws. Many of these women were practising lesbians.

Natalie was fascinated by their appalling language and rebellious behaviour. It gave her pleasure to ring up Sarah and Moshe, who had reached the age of about twenty.

Natalie always amused the two other secretaries in her office. They loved her imitation of the prisoners' voices, and even went so far as to make her banana cakes, in return.

***

After a few months, Natalie's post at the Whittington Hospital came to an end, because a much more experienced secretary was appointed. Her name was Lydia, and she had been working among tuberculosis patients for at least ten years, as well as patients suffering from chest diseases in general.

Natalie approached another agency, whose staff sent her to the University College Hospital in Central London, where she was told to report to the personnel manager, Mrs Judith Anderson, the head of the secretariat there.

"I like all my secretaries to type their correspondence, in the form of letters to consultants first," began Judith. "After that, I like them to type the discharge summaries, which are much longer, and more complicated," she said assertively. "Then I like my girls to bring their work down to my office, so that I can inspect it."

The secretariat was dark and divided into cubicles. Natalie went into one of them and studied the instructions in front of her.

"My name is Namu," said an Indian woman sitting next to her, adding, "You are to do exactly what I tell you to do, not what Judith tells you to do." Namu had a long black plait, reaching her waist.

"I can't do what you tell me to do. I will do precisely what Judith tells me to do," said Natalie.

"Shut up! I'm having a lot of trouble with my mother-in-law. Life isn't easy for me."

"I'm not interested in your blasted bloody mother-in-law. I'm not even interested in you. I'm doing what Judith has told me to do. Leave me alone."

Without preamble, Namu swept all the papers off Natalie's desk.

Natalie spontaneously seized a pair of scissors and cut Namu's plait off at the neck. Namu pressed a button under her desk, which caused Judith to rush upstairs and storm into the secretariat.

"What's going on?" demanded Judith mildly.

Natalie held the severed black plait in her hand and waved it in the air.

"I was provoked," she said lamely.

Judith took Namu's side, because she had worked in the secretariat for five years, whereas Natalie had only worked there for a few days, even though she had implicitly obeyed her orders.

"Would you please ring your agency," said Judith. "Your services are no longer required in this hospital, unless you wish to attend as a patient."

"I did as I was told," replied Natalie.

"I don't care. You caused serious damage, to someone's property."

Later that evening, she phoned Mrs Goulding and poured out her sorrow to her new family.

***

Natalie did not expect to hear from any further employment agencies. Soon, she received a phone call from Sarah, stating that Moshe had successfully proposed to his girlfriend, Rachel, and that the two would be marrying in Jerusalem, within about a month.

Natalie packed a suitcase, containing the appropriate clothing for a Jewish wedding, namely a smart, longish silk dress and matching silk material to cover her head with. She also wore long lace gloves, although these were not entirely necessary.

She was overly excited by the cracking of the light bulb between a piece of white cloth, so much at variance with many Anglican weddings which she had attended in the past.

There was lively singing and dancing throughout the night. Moshe was in his element. Natalie did not go to bed until the small hours. She checked into the King David Hotel, and slept in a dark, lavish bedroom, once occupied by one of the presidents of the United States.

The following morning, she visited Moshe's father's grave, as she had before, and boarded the next plane to London. She then took a taxi to Golders Green. She was exhausted. Her maid, Rhoda, brought her meals in bed, before she felt like receiving any guests.

She no longer sought medical secretarial work, but the only other hospital in which she had disgraced herself, was the Royal Free Hospital, in Hampstead. A patronising doctor, aware of Natalie's knowledge of Russian, asked her the Russian for "You are most welcome here", to say to her new maid. Natalie gave the doctor the Russian for "Have you got a big cunt?".

When the unfortunate doctor got out of the lift, the following morning, most of her teeth were missing, and Natalie delighted in telling her guests the anecdote.

She continued to phone her contacts in Israel from home every morning, and gained a lot of pleasure, speaking to Moshe's mother, Moshe's bride and Moshe himself. She was on the phone for over an hour at times. She had also learned some Hebrew and continued to regard the Gouldings as a second family.

***

Later that week, Natalie received the terrible news that her sister, Hilary, had been taken seriously ill with COVID and pneumonia together. Rhoda had sent for a doctor called Dr Carter, since Dr Festenstein, the much-loved family doctor, was away. Hilary was staying in Natalie's house, and Rhoda was helping to look after her.

Natalie spoke to Dr Carter at length, but had little faith in him, particularly as Hilary was deteriorating. As Dr Carter and Natalie were sitting by Hilary's bedside, the doctor suddenly had hysterical giggles, without cause.

Natalie flew into a rage.

"I'll be organising my sister's funeral shortly! Why the hell are you sitting there sniggering?" she shouted.

Hilary made a belated recovery, however, but Natalie

still felt hostile towards Dr Carter. She grabbed him by the tie and pushed him out of the front door.

"Are you the cunt who urinated against a statue of Sir Winston Churchill?" she shouted, her voice raised, adding, "I'm reporting you for gross negligence."

Dr Carter arranged for a barrister to represent him. At first, he was fairly pleased by the seemingly pleasant-looking appearance of the judge.

The doctor assumed a casual mien and put his hands in his pockets.

"Where are you from?" asked the judge.

"Colchester."

"You can keep your hands in your pockets when you're in Colchester, but kindly do not do so when you're in my court!"

"I apologise, My Lord," ventured Dr Carter.

Suddenly, the judge dropped one of his contact lenses and frenziedly leant forward to retrieve it.

Natalie had just received a spectacular royalty statement and felt a sense of euphoria. She was also overjoyed by the improvement in her sister's health.

"Looking for your black cap, are you, Your Lordship?" she quipped.

The judge was not amused.

"Miss Klein, I'd thank you from refraining from making sick jokes of that nature!" he retorted.

***

Natalie came home after the case. It was budget day, and the Chancellor of the Exchequer had been walking down the street, holding his bright-red dispatch box.

Reporters were following him. For some reason, best known to himself, he looked out of the window of his limousine and photographed two ducks.

Later, the news was being shown on the television. Natalie and Rhoda roared with laughter. "Why on earth did the chancellor have to photograph two ducks like that?" asked Natalie.

***

Natalie's father, Selwyn Klein, was a newspaper proprietor. He was a workaholic and put in a fifteen-hour day.

Although he was kind to his family, his work was paramount. However, his newspaper, *The Daily Echo*, was horribly plagued by printers' strikes, which invariably brought production to a standstill. So distressing were the printers' strikes, that his life was shortened.

Klein was desperate and he felt the need to hire a private detective, to find out who was behind the continuous strikes. He thought it was likely to be one individual, rather than a group of insurgents.

The private detective, a very loyal man called Alex Faulkner, tracked down a left-winger called Blake, within about six weeks, and nicknamed this character, 'Joe the Printer'.

Because this horrible man greatly shortened her father's life, Natalie managed to find out where he lived. He lived alone in Earl's Court. His wife was dead, and he had one son, called Paul, aged eighteen.

Joe the Printer was devoted to Paul, who was a heroin addict, and who was found dead in a public lavatory. It was one evening on Christmas Eve. Joe really looked forward to spending the following day at home with Paul. This was not to be.

A small parcel came through Joe's letter box just before Christmas. It was beautifully wrapped up in red silk.

Joe unwrapped it, thinking that it was his Christmas present from his son. It was not.

In italic writing, under the silk, were the words: "*Happy Christmas, Daddy, with love from Paul.*" There was a syringe, covered with blood, under the silk.

Natalie felt guilty after her deed.

***

She approached her family doctor, Dr Festenstein.

"I've got some idea what you may want, little one," said Festenstein sympathetically, "although what you did was pretty horrible. I'll send you to a man called Dr Alan Cohen. His rooms are in 112 Harley Street."

Dr Cohen was not exactly Natalie's cup of tea. He did not rise to his feet when she entered his consulting room. Also, it was forbidden to smoke in the waiting room. Natalie did not smoke anyway, but she still resented the rule.

An apple-cheeked receptionist eventually told her to come into Dr Cohen's room. A pair of polished Gucci shoes peeped under his desk, which was neat and tidy.

The doctor had a pugnacious jaw, and a healthy complexion. It appeared that he neither drank nor smoked. Natalie noticed a crumpled copy of *The Guardian* in a wastepaper basket on the floor by Dr Cohen's desk.

"You mean to say you take *The Guardian*, and yet you have rooms in Harley Street?" exclaimed Natalie.

Dr Cohen suddenly picked up the paper, and held it in front of Natalie, as if meaning to hide his fucking gear.

"What have you come to see me about?" he asked. His voice was particularly high-pitched.

Natalie told him about her great love for her late father, and her desire to avenge him. She left nothing out and pointed out her need for an eye for an eye and a tooth for a tooth.

She also told the doctor about her friends, Mrs Goulding and her son, Moshe, both of whom lived in Israel, and abided by this axiom.

The doctor said nothing for about three minutes. Eventually, he self-consciously flapped his copy of *The Guardian* in the air.

"That paper is very anti-Semitic," said Natalie, adding, "I've just told you my story at length, and I have left nothing out, particularly about Paul, the heroin addict. What do you think of my story? Do you not think I've behaved impeccably?"

"Your story is absolutely nauseating!" Dr Cohen's voice was even more high-pitched than it had been earlier.

Natalie flew into a rage and banged her fists onto Dr Cohen's desk.

"My father died of a heart attack, caused by the deeds of Joe the Printer and others like him. Did you love your father?"

There was a silence.

"You really are a fucking old woman!" she added.

She stormed out of his consulting room and found her way home.

***

Sometime later, Natalie was invited to a crowded fancy dress party in Hampstead. Many of the guests were in the newspaper business. The costumes were varied. One woman appeared as Elizabeth I, and an overweight man turned up dressed as Oliver Cromwell.

A slightly built woman appeared as Marilyn Monroe, and even spoke with a frail, gentle voice, to imitate the sex siren's vowels.

There were at least 200 guests there, including a figure, who had disguised himself as Hitler. He was wearing a swastika armband, greyish breaches, shiny black boots and even carried a whip.

He was a certain Alan Winterbottom and had been a prominent printer on Natalie's father's paper, before it had folded. He was more militant even, than Joe the Printer had been.

Natalie came as a gondolier, wearing a striped shirt, a navy-blue cap and navy-blue trousers. She overheard the Hitler character saying how broke he was. She approached him and said she had a hundred and fifty pounds to offer him.

She also took advantage of the fact that he appeared both drunk and stoned, before he got into his old navy-blue Ford Focus. He took the wheel and Natalie got into the passenger's seat, by which time it was at least three o'clock in the morning. She covered the swastika armband and forced him to drive as fast as he could, knocking over the sentry who had blocked the car's path.

She pointed out that Winterbottom was to visit the house of a certain Mr Lenin, whose portrait hung on a wall in the hall. She also pointed out that if he were to spit on it, she would give him one hundred and fifty pounds.

He drunkenly asked what the red piece of cloth over the wrought-iron gate represented. "That's Mr Lenin's bath towel, which he's hanging out to dry. If you want to know what that yellow marking in the corner is, that's his family crest. His ancestors are farmers and carpenters."

Winterbottom appeared satisfied. He got out of his car and began to climb over the gate, leading to the Soviet Embassy. A policeman was on the pavement. He asked Winterbottom what he was doing and pointed out that he appeared to be climbing into the Soviet Embassy under the influence.

"Who are you?" he asked mildly.

"Sir Winston Churchill wouldn't have stood for any of this fucking treatment, Officer. I've come to spit on a portrait of Lenin. If you really want to know, I'm someone's aunt," he added inanely.

"Sir Winston Churchill wouldn't have broken into a Soviet Embassy at three o'clock in the morning, using obscene language, cracking a riding whip, and saying he was someone's aunt!"

Natalie realised that she had gone too far. She got into Winterbottom's car and drove off into the distance, leaving Winterbottom's number plates behind her.

In the meantime, Winterbottom tried to get over the gate a second time, rushed up the steps and rang the bell. A guard on the premises briefly bounded forwards, listened to what he had to say, allowed him to carry out his mission, and shot him dead.

The news got into all the papers within a day or two, and warrants were sent out to different addresses, including Natalie's address.

***

Finally, a bored-looking policeman arrived at Natalie's Golders Green house. Rhoda opened the door. It was about eight days later.

"Are you the writer, Natalie Klein?" asked the policeman.

"No, I'll get her. She's upstairs," said Rhoda.

"What can I do for you? Has someone been taken ill?" asked Natalie.

"Don't mess about, Miss Klein. What were you doing early last Saturday morning?"

"I was here writing."

"I see. What are your interests besides writing?"

"Revenge, mainly. I believe in an eye for an eye and a tooth for a tooth, like the allies against the Germans during World War II. That's why I sent that man to the Soviet Embassy in honour of my father."

"Any other interests?"

"Yes. The male sex," replied Natalie pertly.

The policeman was increasingly irritated and exhausted. He didn't wish to pry anymore, although he knew that Natalie had committed a severe felony, particularly where the Soviet Embassy was concerned. Indeed, her actions could easily have led to World War III.

"I think you had better accompany me to the nearest nick," he said mildly.

He cuffed her and lowered her head.

"You'd better get into the car."

"Do you mean the battered old Cortina in the drive?"

The journey did not take long. She was introduced to the desk sergeant, as all the cells were full.

She was notified of the consequences of her deed, and also of her motives for committing it, even if they had resulted in her father's death.

It was not long before she had to appear in the Knightsbridge Crown Court. Her second court appearance. Faithful Festenstein turned up and stated that she was to be treated with two litres of milk in the witness stand, when giving evidence, due to a kidney complaint.

The judge was sympathetic and was also keen on her extraordinary loyalty towards her father, if it meant her extreme eccentricity in many ways.

Natalie sucked up to the judge by calling him "My Lord" throughout her examination instead of "Your Honour", regardless of the fact that she was only speaking in a Crown Court.

Her opposing barrister, Mr Myers, addressed her crisply and almost crudely "What is your address, Miss Klein?"

"74 Golders Close, Edgeware, Middlesex."

"What is your religion?"

"I am a prolific writer and always have been. There is nothing else I believe in, apart from my pills."

"I understand you have always called yourself a professional writer."

"I do not call myself a writer, sir. I am a writer."

"What do you write?"

"Novels, in the form of black comedies."

"Define a black comedy," said Mr Myers rudely.

"It is a novel for literary work, which states that there is a funny side to all things grave," replied Natalie.

Myers tweaked his white tie.

"How many of these novels so-called, have you written?" he asked unpleasantly.

"At least fifty. I am on the verge of my fiftieth."

"Do you only have one publisher, Miss Klein, or more than one? Think before you speak."

"I have one, and always have done."

"What is the name of your publisher?"

"Potemkin Press, Embankment, London SW3."

There was a pause. Myers had not heard of the name before. He was not familiar with publishers, either well known or otherwise.

"Is your publisher at all renowned?" he asked with a sneer.

"Yes," replied Natalie, adding, "most well-known biographers and writers use them. Also, novelists use them in droves."

"I see," said Myers. "I'd like to get to the matter in hand, namely your need to take revenge, all the time.

"Let's begin with your attack on left-wing printers, working on your father's newspapers, namely on a certain 'Joe the Printer', who was alleged to have brought your father to his knees, finally to his death, or so you said.

"You also attacked the father of a heroin addict called Paul."

Natalie giggled. Maybe this was an example of her nervous black humour.

"What are you laughing at, Miss Klein?" asked Mr Myers.

Natalie ignored him.

Mr Myers continued, "Finally, you were responsible for the death of a certain Alan Winterbottom who broke into the Soviet Embassy, at your request, under the influence of drink and drugs, only to be shot dead in the end, by one of the guards. Your actions could have brought about World War III."

Mr Leskin, Natalie's supporting barrister, could take no more.

"My Learned Friend, I really must object," he shouted, at the top of his voice.

"What you have said, while questioning this witness, is a sheer travesty of justice, a waffly and complete and utter farce. Most of Miss Klein's actions are no more than pranks.

"All this time, it has been shown that she was acting in her father's interests and through love of her father alone."

The judge, Mr Hordern, was extremely conservative and supported particularly conservative newspapers.

The jury were divided, however. Some jury members were of the opinion that Natalie's actions were irresponsible and even vicious at times. That is partly why they took so long to reach a verdict.

Natalie was depressed and exhausted as she waited in the dock. She was convinced that she would end up with a jail sentence, particularly as she had been to prison before.

The litres of milk comforted her. Also, many jury members were extremely frustrated by their need to do their groceries shopping as well as to pay their bills, which had become immense. In addition, it was raining heavily. Taxis were hard to come by in that part of London, and most of these wretched people wanted out, for want of better words.

The foreman entered the courtroom and was asked whether a verdict had been reached. He replied that it had, and that Natalie was not guilty of felony of any kind.

The judge, Mr Hordern, stated that, though she was a bit of a prankster, she was a loyal and worthy citizen. In other words, she could walk.

Added to this, Dr Festenstein, who had followed every minute of the case, grabbed his patient by the hand.

"I've got wonderful news for you, Natalie," he stated. "I finally managed to divorce my wife, after several months, as you know. How would you like to come to Israel with me, Mrs Goulding and her family? I may stop becoming a doctor for a while and contribute towards the war effort."

"How on earth would we manage to go without milk?" pleaded Natalie.

"I know the heads of the kitchens at the King David Hotel, which you stayed in before. They will provide us with milk."

"You have to let me think about it," said Natalie.

She went to a nearby cafe and started to write a new book. The cafe was next to a funeral parlour and reminded her of her past and of the days when she worked as a funeral director.

A man in funeral director's clothing took an interest in her.

"Can I help you?" he asked.

"Piss off! I'm trying to write a fucking book. I've already made my funeral arrangements. Another thing, stop smoking that bloody pipe. It's getting into my hair. Next time, perhaps you could bring a tape measure with you."

"You really are very rude," said the funeral director.

"We both are. I am trying to. You can't help it."

Natalie told Festenstein about the conversation. She was still nervous.

"My lovely girl! You will come with me, won't you?"

"I'll try. I really will," she replied.